The Boy with the Moon on his Forehead
and
Other Folk-Tales

The Boy with the Moon on his Forehead and Other Folk-Tales

Lal Behari Dey

Illustrations by
Warwick Goble

HAWK PRESS

Published by

Hawk Press
4836/24, Ansari Road, Daryaganj
New Delhi – 110 002
Phones : 9643330713, +91-11-23278618, +91-11-35676207
E-mail: thehawkpress@gmail.com
www.thehawkpress.com

Contents

TO
RICHARD CARNAC TEMPLE
CAPTAIN, BENGAL STAFF CORPS
F.R.G.S., M.R.A.S., M.A.I., ETC.
WHO FIRST SUGGESTED TO THE WRITER
THE IDEA OF COLLECTING
THESE TALES
AND WHO IS DOING SO MUCH
IN THE CAUSE OF INDIAN FOLK-LORE
THIS LITTLE BOOK
IS INSCRIBED

Preface

In my Peasant Life in Bengal I make the peasant boy Govinda spend some hours every evening in listening to stories told by an old woman, who was called Sambhu's mother, and who was the best story-teller in the village. On reading that passage, Captain R. C. Temple, of the Bengal Staff Corps, son of the distinguished Indian administrator Sir Richard Temple, wrote to me to say how interesting it would be to get a collection of those unwritten stories which old women in India recite to little children in the evenings, and to ask whether I could not make such a collection. As I was no stranger to the Mährchen of the Brothers Grimm, to the Norse Tales so admirably told by Dasent, to Arnason's Icelandic Stories translated by Powell, to the Highland Stories done into English by Campbell, and to the fairy stories collected by other writers, and as I believed that the collection suggested would be a contribution, however slight, to that daily increasing literature of folk-lore and comparative mythology which, like comparative philosophy, proves that the swarthy and half-naked peasant on the banks of the Ganges is a cousin, albeit of the hundredth remove, to the fair-skinned and well-dressed

Englishman on the banks of the Thames, I readily caught up the idea and cast about for materials. But where was an old story-telling woman to be got? I had myself, when a little boy, heard hundreds—it would be no exaggeration to say thousands—of fairy tales from that same old woman, Sambhu's mother—for she was no fictitious person; she actually lived in the flesh and bore that name; but I had nearly forgotten those stories, at any rate they had all got confused in my head, the tail of one story being joined to the head of another, and the head of a third to the tail of a fourth.

How I wished that poor Sambhu's mother had been alive! But she had gone long, long ago, to that bourne from which no traveller returns, and her son Sambhu, too, had followed her thither. After a great deal of search I found my Gammer Grethel—though not half so old as the Frau Viehmännin of Hesse-Cassel—in the person of a Bengali Christian woman, who, when a little girl and living in her heathen home, had heard many stories from her old grandmother. She was a good story-teller, but her stock was not large; and after I had heard ten from her I had to look about for fresh sources. An old Brahman told me two stories; an old barber, three; an old servant of mine told me two; and the rest I heard from another old Brahman. None of my authorities knew English; they all told the stories in Bengali, and I translated them into English when I came home. I heard many more stories than those contained in the following pages; but I rejected a great many, as they appeared to me to contain spurious additions to the original stories which I had heard when a boy. I have reason to believe that the stories given in this book are a genuine sample of the old old stories told by old Bengali women from age to age through a hundred generations.

Sambhu's mother used always to end every one of her stories—and every orthodox Bengali story-teller does the same—with repeating the following formula:—

Thus my story endeth,
The Natiya-thorn withereth.
"Why, O Natiya-thorn, dost wither?"
"Why does thy cow on me browse?"
"Why, O cow, dost thou browse?"
"Why does thy neat-herd not tend me?"
"Why, O neat-herd, dost not tend the cow?"
"Why does thy daughter-in-law not give me rice?"
"Why, O daughter-in-law, dost not give rice?"
"Why does my child cry?"
"Why, O child, dost thou cry?"
"Why does the ant bite me?"
"Why, O ant, dost thou bite?"
Koot! koot! koot!

What these lines mean, why they are repeated at the end of every story, and what the connection is of the several parts to one another, I do not know. Perhaps the whole is a string of nonsense purposely put together to amuse little children.

Lal Behari Day
Hooghly College,
February 27, 1883.

1

The Story of a Hiraman[1]

here was a fowler who had a wife. The fowler's wife said to her husband one day, "My dear, I'll tell you the reason why we are always in want. It is because you sell every bird you catch by your rods, whereas if we sometimes eat some of the birds you catch, we are sure to have better luck. I propose therefore that whatever bird or birds you bag to-day we do not sell, but dress and eat." The fowler agreed to his wife's proposal, and went out a-bird-catching. He went about from wood to wood with his limed rods, accompanied by his wife, but in vain. Somehow or other they did not succeed in catching any bird till near sundown. But just as they were returning homewards they caught a beautiful hiraman. The fowler's wife, taking the bird in her hand and feeling it all over, said, "What a small bird this is! how much meat can it have? There is no use in killing it." The hiraman said, "Mother, do not kill me, but take me to the king, and you will get a large sum of money by selling me." The fowler and his wife were greatly taken aback on hearing the bird speak, and they asked the bird what price they should set upon it. The hiraman answered, "Leave that to me; take me to the king and offer me for sale; and when the king asks my price, say, 'The bird will tell its own price,' and then I'll mention a large sum." The fowler accordingly went the next day to the king's palace, and offered the bird for sale. The king, delighted with the beauty of the bird, asked the fowler what he would take for it. The fowler said, "O great king, the bird will tell its own price." "What! can the bird speak?" asked the king. "Yes, my lord; be pleased to ask the bird its price," replied the fowler. The king, half in jest and half in seriousness, said, "Well, hiraman, what is your price?" The hiraman answered, "Please your majesty, my price is ten thousand rupees. Do not think that the price is too high. Count out the money for the fowler, for I'll be of the greatest service to your majesty." "What service can you be of to me, hiraman?" asked the king. "Your majesty will see that in due time," replied the hiraman. The king, surprised beyond measure at hearing the hiraman talk, and talk so sensibly, took the bird, and ordered his treasurer to tell down the sum of ten thousand rupees to the fowler.

The king had six queens, but he was so taken up with the bird that he almost forgot that they lived; at any rate, his days and nights were spent in the company, not of the queens, but of the bird. The hiraman not only replied intelligently to every question the king put, but it recited to him the names of the three hundred and thirty millions of the gods of the Hindu pantheon, the hearing of which is always regarded as an act of piety. The queens felt that they were neglected by the king, became jealous of the bird, and determined to kill it. It was long before they got an opportunity, as the bird was the king's inseparable companion. One day the king went out a-hunting, and he was to be away from the palace for two days. The six queens determined to avail themselves of the opportunity and put an end to the life of the bird. They said to one another, "Let us go and ask the bird which of us is the ugliest in his estimation, and she whom he pronounces the ugliest shall strangle the bird." Thus resolved, they all went into the room where the bird was; but before the queens could put any questions the bird so sweetly and so piously recited the names of the gods and goddesses, that the hearts of them all were melted into tenderness, and they came away without accomplishing their purpose. The following day, however, their evil genius returned, and they called themselves a thousand fools for having been diverted from their purpose. They therefore determined to steel their hearts against all pity, and to kill the bird without delay. They all went into the room, and said to the bird, "O hiraman, you are a very wise bird, we hear, and your judgments are all right; will you please tell us which of us is the handsomest and which the ugliest?" The bird, knowing the evil design of the queens, said to them, "How can I answer your questions remaining in this cage? In order to pronounce a correct judgment I must look minutely on every limb of you all, both in front and behind. If you wish to know my opinion you must set me free." The women were at first afraid of setting the bird free lest it should fly away; but on second thoughts they set it free after shutting all the doors and windows of the room. The bird, on examining the room, saw that it had a water-passage through which it was possible to escape. When the question was repeated several times by the queens, the bird said, "The beauty of not one of you can be compared to the beauty of the little toe of the lady that lives beyond the seven oceans and the thirteen rivers." The queens, on hearing their beauty spoken of in such slighting terms, became exceedingly furious, and rushed towards the bird to tear it in pieces; but before they could get at it, it escaped through the water-passage, and took shelter in a wood-cutter's hut which was hard by.

The next day the king returned home from hunting, and not finding the hiraman on its perch became mad with grief. He asked the queens, and they told him that they knew nothing about it. The king wept day and night for the bird, as he loved it much. His ministers became afraid lest his reason should give way, for he used every hour of the day to weep, saying, "O my hiraman! O my hiraman! where art thou gone?" Proclamation was made by beat of drum throughout the kingdom to the effect that if any person could produce before the king his pet hiraman he would be rewarded with ten thousand rupees. The wood-cutter, rejoiced at the idea of becoming independent for life, produced the precious bird and obtained the reward. The king, on hearing from the parrot that the queens had attempted to kill it, became mad with rage. He ordered them to be driven away from the palace and put in a desert place without food. The king's order was obeyed, and it was rumoured after a few days that the poor queens were all devoured by wild beasts.

After some time the king said to the parrot, "Hiraman, you said to the queens that the beauty of none of them could be compared to the beauty of even the little toe of the lady who lives on the other side of the seven oceans and thirteen rivers. Do you know of any means by which I can get at that lady?"

Hiraman. Of course I do. I can take your majesty to the door of the palace in which that lady of peerless beauty lives; and if your majesty will abide by my counsel, I will undertake to put that lady into your arms.

King. I will do whatever you tell me. What do you wish me to do?

Hiraman. What is required is a pakshiraj.[2] If you can procure a horse of that species, you can ride upon it, and in no time we shall cross the seven oceans and thirteen rivers, and stand at the door of the lady's palace.

King. I have, as you know, a large stud of horses; we can now go and see if there are any pakshirajes amongst them.

The king and the hiraman went to the royal stables and examined all the horses. The hiraman passed by all the fine-looking horses and those of high mettle, and alighted upon a wretched-looking lean pony, and said, "Here is the horse I want. It is a horse of the genuine pakshiraj breed, but it must be fed full six months with the finest grain before it can answer our purpose." The king accordingly put that pony in a stable by itself and himself saw every day that it was fed with the finest grain that could be got in the kingdom. The pony rapidly improved in appearance, and at the end of six months the hiraman pronounced it fit for service. The parrot then told the king to order the royal silversmith to make some khais[3] of silver. A large quantity of silver khais was made in a short time. When about to start on their aërial journey the hiraman said to the king, "I have one request to make. Please whip the horse only once at starting. If you whip him more than once, we shall not be able to reach the palace, but stick mid-way. And when we return homewards after capturing the lady, you are also to whip the horse only once; if you whip him more than once, we shall come only half the way and remain there." The king then got upon the pakshiraj with the hiraman and the silver khais and gently whipped the animal once. The horse shot through the air with the speed of lightning, passed over many countries, kingdoms, and empires, crossed the oceans and thirteen rivers, and alighted in the evening at the gate of a beautiful palace.

Now, near the palace-gate there stood a lofty tree. The hiraman told the king to put the horse in the stable hard by, and then to climb into the tree and remain there concealed. The hiraman took the silver khais, and with its beak began dropping khai after khai from the foot of the tree, all through the corridors and passages, up to the door of the bedchamber of the lady of peerless beauty. After doing this, the hiraman perched upon the tree where the king was concealed. Some hours after midnight, the maid-servant of the lady, who slept in the same room with her, wishing to come out, opened the door and noticed the silver khais lying there. She took up a few of them, and not knowing what they were, showed them to her lady. The lady, admiring the little silver bullets, and wondering how they could have got there, came out of her room and began picking them up. She saw a regular stream of them apparently issuing from near the door of her room, and proceeding she knew not how far. She went on picking up in a basket the bright, shining khais all through the corridors and passages, till she came to the foot of the tree. No sooner did the lady of peerless beauty come to the foot of the tree than the king, agreeably to instructions previously given to him by the hiraman, alighted from the tree and caught hold of the lady. In a moment she was put upon the horse along with himself. At that moment the hiraman sat upon the shoulder of the king, the king gently whipped the horse once, and they all were whirled through the air with the speed of lightning. The king, wishing to reach home soon with the precious prize, and forgetful of the instructions of the hiraman, whipped the horse again; on which the horse at once alighted on the outskirts of what seemed a dense forest. "What have you done, O king?" shouted out the hiraman. "Did I not tell you not to whip the horse more than once? You have whipped him twice, and we are done for. We may meet with our death here." But the thing was done, and it could not be helped. The pakshiraj became powerless; and the party could not proceed homewards. They dismounted; but they could not see anywhere the habitations of men. They ate some fruits and roots, and slept that night there upon the ground.

Next morning it so chanced that the king of that country came to that forest to hunt. As he was pursuing a stag, whom he had pierced with an arrow, he came across the king and the lady of peerless beauty. Struck with the matchless beauty of the lady, he wished to seize her. He whistled, and in a moment his attendants flocked around him. The lady was made a captive, and her lover, who had brought her from her house on the other side of the seven oceans and thirteen rivers, was not put to death, but his eyes were put out, and he was left alone in the forest—alone, and yet not alone, for the good hiraman was with him.

*"The lady, king, and hiraman all reached the king's capital
safe and sound"*

The lady of peerless beauty was taken into the king's palace, as well as the pony of her lover. The lady said to the king that he must not come near her for six months, in consequence of a vow which she had taken, and which would be completed in that period of time. She mentioned six months, as that period would be necessary for recruiting the constitution of the pakshiraj. As the lady professed to engage every day in religious ceremonies, in consequence of her vow, a separate house was assigned to her, where she took the pakshiraj and fed him with the choicest grain. But everything would be fruitless if the lady did not meet the hiraman. But how is she to get a sight of that bird? She adopted the following expedient. She ordered her servants to scatter on the roof of her house heaps of paddy, grain, and all sorts of pulse for the refreshment of birds. The consequence was, that thousands of the feathery race came to the roof to partake of the abundant feast. The lady was every day on the look out for her hiraman. The hiraman, meanwhile, was in great distress in the forest. He had to take care not only of himself, but of the now blinded king. He plucked some ripe fruits in the forest, and gave them to the king to eat, and he ate of them himself. This was the manner of hiraman's life. The other birds of the forest spoke thus to the parrot— "O hiraman, you have a miserable life of it in this forest. Why don't you come with us to an abundant feast provided for us by a pious lady, who scatters many maunds of pulse on the roof of her house for the benefit of our race? We go there early in the morning and return in the evening, eating our fill along with thousands of other birds." The hiraman resolved to accompany them next morning, shrewdly suspecting more in the lady's charity to birds than the other birds thought there was in it. The hiraman saw the lady, and had a long chat with her about the health of the blinded king, the means of curing his blindness, and about her escape. The plan adopted was as follows: The pony would be ready for aerial flight in a short time—for a great part of the six months had already elapsed; and the king's blindness could be cured if the hiraman could procure from the chicks of the bihangama and bihangami birds, who had their nest on the tree at the gate of the lady's palace beyond the seven oceans and thirteen rivers, a quantity of their ordure, fresh and hot, and apply it to the eyeballs of the blinded king. The following morning the hiraman started on his errand of mercy, remained at night on the tree at the gate of the palace beyond the seven oceans and thirteen rivers, and early the next morning waited below the nest of the birds with a leaf on his beak, into which dropped the ordure of the chicks. That moment the hiraman flew across the oceans and rivers, came to the forest, and applied the precious balm to the sightless sockets of the king. The king opened his eyes and saw. In a few days the pakshiraj was in proper trim. The lady escaped to the forest and took the king up; and the lady, king, and hiraman all reached the king's capital safe and sound. The king and the lady were united together in wedlock. They lived many years together happily, and begat sons and daughters; and the beautiful hiraman was always with them reciting the names of the three hundred and thirty millions of gods.

1. "Hiraman (from harit, green, and mani, a gem), the name of a beautiful species of parrot, a native of the Molucca Islands (Psittacus sinensis)."—Carey's Dictionary of the Bengalee Language, vol. ii. part iii. p. 1537.
2. Winged horse, literally, the king of birds.
3. Khai is fried paddy.

2

The Origin of Rubies

There was a certain king who died leaving four sons behind him with his queen. The queen was passionately fond of the youngest of the princes. She gave him the best robes, the best horses, the best food, and the best furniture. The other three princes became exceedingly jealous of their youngest brother, and conspiring against him and their mother, made them live in a separate house, and took possession of the estate. Owing to overindulgence, the youngest prince had become very wilful. He never listened to any one, not even to his mother, but had his own way in everything. One day he went with his mother to bathe in the river. A large boat was riding there at anchor. None of the boatmen were in it. The prince went into the boat, and told his mother to come into it. His mother besought him to get down from the boat, as it did not belong to him. But the prince said, "No, mother, I am not coming down; I mean to go on a voyage, and if you wish to come with me, then delay not but come up at once, or I shall be off in a trice." The queen besought the prince to do no such thing, but to come down instantly. But the prince gave no heed to what she said, and began to take up the anchor. The queen went up into the boat in great haste; and the moment she was on board the boat started, and falling into the current passed on swiftly like an arrow. The boat went on and on till it reached the sea. After it had gone many furlongs into the open sea, the boat came near a whirlpool, where the prince saw a great many rubies of monstrous size floating on the waters. Such large rubies no one had ever seen, each being in value equal to the wealth of seven kings. The prince caught hold of half a dozen of those rubies, and put them on board. His mother said, "Darling, don't take up those red balls; they must belong to somebody who has been shipwrecked, and we may be taken up as thieves." At the repeated entreaties of his mother the prince threw them into the sea, keeping only one tied up in his clothes. The boat then drifted towards the coast, and the queen and the prince arrived at a certain port where they landed.

The port where they landed was not a small place; it was a large city, the capital of a great king. Not far from the place, the queen and her son hired a hut where they lived. As the prince was yet a boy, he was fond of playing at marbles. When the children of the king came out to play on a lawn before the palace, our young prince joined them. He had no marbles, but he played with the ruby which he had in his possession. The ruby was so hard that it broke every taw against which it struck. The daughter of the king, who used to watch the games from a balcony of the palace, was astonished to see a brilliant red ball in the hand of the strange lad, and wanted to take possession of it. She told her father that a boy of the street had an uncommonly bright stone in his possession which she must

have, or else she would starve herself to death. The king ordered
his servants to bring to him the lad with the precious stone.
When the boy was brought, the king wondered at the largeness
and brilliancy of the ruby. He had never seen anything like
it. He doubted whether any king of any country in the world
possessed so great a treasure. He asked the lad where he had got
it. The lad replied that he got it from the sea. The king offered a
thousand rupees for the ruby, and the lad not knowing its value
readily parted with it for that sum. He went with the money
to his mother, who was not a little frightened, thinking that
her son had stolen the money from some rich man's house. She
became quiet, however, on being assured that the money was
given to him by the king in exchange for the red ball which he
had picked up in the sea.

The king's daughter, on getting the ruby, put it in her hair, and,
standing before her pet parrot, said to the bird, "Oh, my darling
parrot, don't I look very beautiful with this ruby in my hair?"
The parrot replied, "Beautiful! you look quite hideous with it!
What princess ever puts only one ruby in her hair? It would be
somewhat feasible if you had two at least." Stung with shame at
the reproach cast in her teeth by the parrot, the princess went
into the grief-chamber of the palace, and would neither eat nor
drink. The king was not a little concerned when he heard that
his daughter had gone into the grief-chamber. He went to her,
and asked her the cause of her grief. The princess told the king
what her pet parrot had said, and added, "Father, if you do not
procure for me another ruby like this, I'll put an end to my life
by mine own hands." The king was overwhelmed with grief.
Where was he to get another ruby like it? He doubted whether
another like it could be found in the whole world. He ordered

the lad who had sold the ruby to be brought into his presence. "Have you, young man," asked the king, "another ruby like the one you sold me?" The lad replied, "No, I have not got one. Why, do you want another? I can give you lots, if you wish to have them. They are to be found in a whirlpool in the sea, far, far away. I can go and fetch some for you." Amazed at the lad's reply, the king offered rich rewards for procuring only another ruby of the same sort.

The lad went home and said to his mother that he must go to sea again to fetch some rubies for the king. The woman was quite frightened at the idea, and begged him not to go.

"'What princess ever puts only one ruby in her hair?'"

But the lad was resolved on going, and nothing could prevent him from carrying out his purpose. He accordingly went alone on board that same vessel which had brought him and his mother, and set sail. He reached the whirlpool, from near which he had formerly picked up the rubies. This time, however, he determined to go to the exact spot whence the rubies were coming out. He went to the centre of the whirlpool, where he saw a gap reaching to the bottom of the ocean. He dived into it, leaving his boat to wheel round the whirlpool. When he reached the bottom of the ocean he saw there a beautiful palace. He went inside. In the central room of the palace there was the god Siva, with his eyes closed, and absorbed apparently in intense meditation. A few feet above Siva's head was a platform, on which lay a young lady of exquisite beauty. The prince went to the platform and saw that the head of the lady was separated from her body. Horrified at the sight, he did not know what to make of it. He saw a stream of blood trickling from the severed head, falling upon the matted head of Siva, and running into the ocean in the form of rubies. After a little two small rods, one of silver and one of gold, which were lying near the head of the lady, attracted his eyes. As he took up the rods in his hands, the golden rod accidentally fell upon the head, on which the head immediately joined itself to the body, and the lady got up. Astonished at the sight of a human being, the lady asked the prince who he was and how he had got there. After hearing the story of the prince's adventures, the lady said, "Unhappy young man, depart instantly from this place; for when Siva finishes his meditations he will turn you to ashes by a single glance of his eyes." The young man, however, would not go except in her company, as he was over head and ears in love with the beautiful lady. At last they both contrived to run away from the palace, and coming up to the surface of the ocean they climbed into the boat near the centre of the whirlpool, and sailed away towards land, having previously laden the vessel with a cargo of rubies. The wonder of the prince's mother at seeing the beautiful damsel may be well imagined. Early next morning the prince sent a basin full of big rubies, through a servant. The king was astonished beyond measure. His daughter, on getting the rubies, resolved on marrying the wonderful lad who had made a present of them to her. Though the prince had a wife, whom he had brought up from the depths of the ocean, he consented to have a second wife. They were accordingly married, and lived happily for years, begetting sons and daughters.

"Coming up to the surface they climbed into the boat"

3

The Match-making Jackal

Once on a time there lived a weaver, whose ancestors were very rich, but whose father had wasted the property which he had inherited in riotous living. He was born in a palace-like house, but he now lived in a miserable hut. He had no one in the world, his parents and all his relatives having died. Hard by the hut was the lair of a jackal. The jackal, remembering the wealth and grandeur of the weaver's forefathers, had compassion on him, and one day coming to him, said, "Friend weaver, I see what a wretched life you are leading. I have a good mind to improve your condition. I'll try and marry you to the daughter of the king of this country." "I become the king's son-in-law!" replied the weaver; "that will take place only when the sun rises in the west." "You doubt my power?" rejoined the jackal; "you will see, I'll bring it about."

The next morning the jackal started for the king's city, which was many miles off. On the way he entered a plantation of the Piper betel plant, and plucked a large quantity of its leaves. He reached the capital, and contrived to get inside the palace. On the premises of the palace was a tank in which the ladies of the king's household performed their morning and afternoon ablutions. At the entrance of that tank the jackal laid himself down. The daughter of the king happened to come just at the time to bathe, accompanied by her maids. The princess was not a little struck at seeing the jackal lying down at the entrance. She told her maids to drive the jackal away. The jackal rose as if from sleep, and instead of running away, opened his bundle of betel-leaves, put some into his mouth, and began chewing them. The princess and her maids were not a little astonished at the sight. They said among themselves, "What an uncommon jackal is this! From what country can he have come? A jackal chewing betel-leaves! why thousands of men and women of this city cannot indulge in that luxury. He must have come from a wealthy land." The princess asked the jackal, "Sivalu!¹ from what country do you come? It must be a very prosperous country where the jackals chew betel-leaves. Do other animals in your country chew betel-leaves?" "Dearest princess," replied the jackal, "I come from a land flowing with milk and honey. Betel-leaves are as plentiful in my country as the grass in your fields. All animals in my country—cows, sheep, dogs—chew betel-leaves. We want no good thing." "Happy is the country," said the princess, "where there is such plenty, and thrice happy the king who rules in it!" "As for our king," said the jackal, "he is the richest king in the world. His palace is like the heaven of Indra. I have seen your palace here; it is a miserable hut compared to the palace of our king." The princess, whose curiosity was excited to the utmost pitch, hastily went through her bath, and going to the apartments of the queen-mother, told her of the wonderful jackal lying at the entrance of the tank. Her curiosity being excited, the jackal was sent for. When the jackal stood in the presence of the queen, he began munching the betel-leaves. "You come," said the queen, "from a very rich country. Is your king married?" "Please your majesty, our king is not married. Princesses from distant parts of the world tried to get married to him, but he rejected them all. Happy will that princess be whom our king condescends to marry!" "Don't you think, Sivalu," asked the queen, "that my daughter is as beautiful as a Peri, and that she is fit to be the wife of the proudest king in the world?" "I quite think," said the jackal, "that the princess is exceedingly handsome; indeed, she is the handsomest princess I have ever seen; but I don't know whether our king will have a liking for her." "Liking for my daughter!" said the queen, "you have only to paint her to him as she is, and he is sure to turn mad with love. To be serious, Sivalu, I am anxious to get my daughter married. Many princes have sought her hand, but I am unwilling to give her to any of them, as they are not the sons of great kings. But your king seems to be a great king. I can have no objection to making him my son-in-law." The queen sent word to the king, requesting him to come and see the jackal. The king came and saw the jackal, heard him describe the wealth and pomp of the king of his country, and expressed himself not unwilling to give away his daughter in marriage to him.

"The jackal ... opened his bundle of betel-leaves, put some into his mouth, and began chewing them"

The jackal after this returned to the weaver and said to him, "O lord of the loom, you are the luckiest man in the world; it is all settled; you are to become the son-in-law of a great king. I have told them that you are yourself a great king, and you must behave yourself as one. You must do just as I instruct you, otherwise your fortune will not only not be made, but both you and I will be put to death." "I'll do just as you bid me," said the weaver. The shrewd jackal drew in his own mind a plan of the method of procedure he should adopt, and after a few days went back to the palace of the king in the same manner in which he had gone before, that is to say, chewing betel-leaves and lying down at the entrance of the tank on the premises of the palace. The king and queen were glad to see him, and eagerly asked him as to the success of his mission. The jackal said, "In order to relieve your minds I may tell you at once that my mission has been so far successful. If you only knew the infinite trouble I have had in persuading his Majesty, my sovereign, to make up his mind to marry your daughter, you would give me no end of thanks. For a long time he would not hear of it, but gradually I brought him round. You have now only to fix an auspicious day for the celebration of the solemn rite. There is one bit of advice, however, which I, as your friend, would give you. It is this. My master is so great a king that if he were to come to you in state, attended by all his followers, his horses and his elephants, you would find it impossible to accommodate them all in your palace or in your city. I would therefore propose that our king should come to your city, not in state, but in a private manner; and that you send to the outskirts of your city your own elephants, horses, and conveyances, to bring him and only a few of his followers to your palace." "Many thanks, wise Sivalu, for this advice. I could not possibly make accommodation in my city for the followers of so great a king as your master is. I should be very glad if he did not come in state; and trust you will use your influence to persuade him to come in a private manner; for I should be ruined if he came in state." The jackal then gravely said, "I will do my best in the matter," and then returned to his own village, after the royal astrologer had fixed an auspicious day for the wedding.

On his return the jackal busied himself with making preparations for the great ceremony. As the weaver was clad in tatters, he told him to go to the washermen of the village and borrow from them a suit of clothes. As for himself, he went to the king of his race, and told him that on a certain day he would like one thousand jackals to accompany him to a certain place. He went to the king of crows, and begged that his corvine majesty would be pleased to allow one thousand of his black subjects to accompany him on a certain day to a certain place. He preferred a similar petition to the king of paddy-birds.

At last the great day arrived. The weaver arrayed himself in the clothes which he had borrowed from the village washermen. The jackal made his appearance, accompanied by a train of a thousand jackals, a thousand crows, and a thousand paddy-birds. The nuptial procession started on their journey, and towards sundown arrived within two miles of the king's palace. There the jackal told his friends, the thousand jackals, to set up a loud howl; at his bidding the thousand crows cawed their loudest; while the hoarse screechings of the thousand paddy-birds furnished a suitable accompaniment. The effect may be imagined. They all together made a noise the like of which had never been heard since the world began. While this unearthly noise was going on, the jackal himself hastened to the palace, and asked the king whether he thought he would be able to accommodate the wedding-party, which was about two miles distant, and whose noise was at that moment sounding in his ears. The king said "Impossible, Sivalu; from the sound of the procession I infer there must be at least one hundred thousand souls. How is it possible to accommodate so many guests? Please, so arrange that the bridegroom only will come to my house." "Very well," said the jackal; "I told you at the beginning that you would not be able to accommodate all the attendants of my august master. I'll do as you wish. My master will alone come in undress. Send a horse for the purpose." The jackal, accompanied by a horse and groom, came to the place where his friend the weaver was, thanked the thousand jackals, the thousand crows, and the thousand paddy-birds, for their valuable services, and told them all to go away, while he himself, and the weaver on horseback, wended their way to the king's palace. The bridal party, waiting in the palace, were greatly disappointed at the personal appearance of the weaver; but the jackal told them that his master had purposely put on a mean dress, as his would-be father-in-law declared himself unable to accommodate the bridegroom and his attendants coming in state. The royal priests now began the interesting ceremony, and the nuptial knot was tied for ever. The bridegroom seldom opened his lips, agreeably to the instructions of the jackal, who was afraid lest his speech should betray him. At night when he was lying in bed he began to count the beams and rafters of the room, and said audibly, "This beam will make a first-rate loom, that other a capital beam, and that yonder an excellent sley." The princess, his bride, was not a little astonished. She began to think in her mind, "Is the man, to whom they have tied me, a king or a weaver? I am afraid he is the latter; otherwise why should he be talking of weaver's loom, beam, and sley? Ah, me! is this what the fates keep in store for me?" In the morning the princess related to the queen-mother the weaver's soliloquy. The king and queen, not a little surprised at this recital, took the jackal to task about it. The ready-witted jackal at once said, "Your Majesty need not be surprised at my august master's soliloquy. His palace is surrounded by a population of seven hundred families of the best weavers in the world, to whom he has given rent-free lands, and whose welfare he continually seeks. It must have been in one of his philanthropic moods that he uttered the soliloquy which has taken your Majesty by surprise." The jackal, however, now felt that it was high time for himself and the weaver to decamp with the princess, since the proverbial simplicity of his friend of the loom might any moment involve him in danger. The jackal therefore represented to the king, that weighty affairs of state would not permit his august master to spend another day in the palace; that he should start for his kingdom that very day with his bride; and his master was resolved to travel incognito on foot, only the princess, now the queen, should leave the city in a palki. After a great deal of yea and nay, the king and queen at last consented to the proposal. The party came to the outskirts of the weaver's village; the palki bearers were sent away; and the princess, who asked where her husband's palace was, was made to walk on foot. The weaver's hut was soon reached, and the jackal, addressing the princess, said, "This, madam, is your husband's palace." The princess began to beat her forehead with the palms of her hands in sheer despair. "Ah, me! is this the husband whom Prajapati[2] intended for me? Death would have been a thousand times better."

As there was nothing for it, the princess soon got reconciled to her fate. She, however, determined to make her husband rich, especially as she knew the secret of becoming rich. One day she told her husband to get for her a pice-worth of flour. She put a little water in the flour, and smeared her body with the paste. When the paste dried on her body, she began wiping the paste with her fingers; and as the paste fell in small balls from her body, it got turned into gold. She repeated this process every day for some time, and thus got an immense quantity of gold. She soon became mistress of more gold than is to be found in the coffers of any king. With this gold she employed a whole army of masons, carpenters and architects, who in no time built one of the finest palaces in the world. Seven hundred families of weavers were sought for and settled round about the palace. After this she wrote a letter to her father to say that she was sorry he had not favoured her with a visit since the day of her marriage, and that she would be delighted if he now came to see her and her husband. The king agreed to come, and a day was fixed. The princess made great preparations against the day of her father's arrival. Hospitals were established in several parts of the town for diseased, sick, and infirm animals. The beasts in thousands were made to chew betel-leaves on the wayside. The streets were covered with Cashmere shawls for her father and his attendants to walk on. There was no end of the display of wealth and grandeur. The king and queen arrived in state, and were infinitely delighted at the apparently boundless riches of their son-in-law. The jackal now appeared on the scene, and saluting the king and queen, said—"Did I not tell you?"

1. A name for a jackal, not unlike Reynard in Europe.
2. The god who presides over marriages.

4

The Boy with the Moon on his Forehead

There was a certain king who had six queens, none of whom bore children. Physicians, holy sages, mendicants, were consulted, countless drugs were had recourse to, but all to no purpose. The king was disconsolate. His ministers told him to marry a seventh wife; and he was accordingly on the look out.

In the royal city there lived a poor old woman who used to pick up cow-dung from the fields, make it into cakes, dry them in the sun, and sell them in the market for fuel. This was her only means of subsistence. This old woman had a daughter exquisitely beautiful. Her beauty excited the admiration of every one that saw her; and it was solely in consequence of her surpassing beauty that three young ladies, far above her in rank and station, contracted friendship with her. Those three young ladies were the daughter of the king's minister, the daughter of a wealthy merchant, and the daughter of the royal priest. These three young ladies, together with the daughter of the poor old woman, were one day bathing in a tank not far from the palace. As they were performing their ablutions, each dwelt on her own good qualities. "Look here, sister," said the minister's daughter, addressing the merchant's daughter, "the man that marries me will be a happy man, for he will not have to buy clothes for me. The cloth which I once put on never gets soiled, never gets old, never tears." The merchant's daughter said, "And my husband too will be a happy man, for the fuel which I use in cooking never gets turned into ashes. The same fuel serves from day to day, from year to year." "And my husband will also become a happy man," said the daughter of the royal chaplain, "for the rice which I cook one day never gets finished, and when we have all eaten, the same quantity which was first cooked remains always in the pot." The daughter of the poor old woman said in her turn, "And the man that marries me will also be happy, for I shall give birth to twin children, a son and a daughter. The daughter will be divinely fair, and the son will have the moon on his forehead and stars on the palms of his hands."

The above conversation was overheard by the king, who, as he was on the look out for a seventh queen, used to skulk about in places where women met together. The king thus thought in his mind—"I don't care a straw for the girl whose clothes never tear and never get old; neither do I care for the other girl whose fuel is never consumed; nor for the third girl whose rice never fails in the pot. But the fourth girl is quite charming! She will give birth to twin children, a son and a daughter; the daughter will be divinely fair, and the son will have the moon on his forehead and stars on the palms of his hands. That is the girl I want. I'll make her my wife."

On making inquiries on the same day, the king found that the fourth girl was the daughter of a poor old woman who picked up cow-dung from the fields; but though there was thus an infinite disparity in rank, he determined to marry her. On the very same day he sent for the poor old woman. She, poor thing, was quite frightened when she saw a messenger of the king standing at the door of her hut. She thought that the king had sent for her to punish her, because, perhaps, she had some day unwittingly picked up the dung of the king's cattle. She went to the palace, and was admitted into the king's private chamber. The king asked her whether she had a very fair daughter, and whether that daughter was the friend of his own minister's and priest's daughters. When the woman answered in the affirmative, he said to her, "I will marry your daughter, and make her my queen." The woman hardly believed her own ears—the thing was so strange. He, however, solemnly declared to her that he had made up his mind, and was determined to marry her daughter. It was soon known in the capital that the king was going to marry the daughter of the old woman who picked up cow-dung in the fields. When the six queens heard the news, they would not believe it, till the king himself told them that the news was true. They thought that the king had somehow got mad. They reasoned with him thus—"What folly, what madness, to marry a girl who is not fit to be our maid-servant! And you expect us to treat her as our equal—a girl whose mother goes about picking up cow-dung in the fields! Surely, my lord, you are beside yourself!" The king's purpose, however, remained unshaken. The royal astrologer was called, and an auspicious day was fixed for the celebration of the king's marriage. On the appointed day the royal priest tied the marital knot, and the daughter of the poor old picker-up of cow-dung in the fields became the seventh and best beloved queen.

Some time after the celebration of the marriage, the king went for six months to another part of his dominions. Before setting out he called to him the seventh queen, and said to her, "I am going away to another part of my dominions for six months. Before the expiration of that period I expect you to be confined. But I should like to be present with you at the time, as your enemies may do mischief. Take this golden bell and hang it in your room. When the pains of childbirth come upon you, ring this bell, and I will be with you in a moment in whatever part of my dominions I may be at the time. Remember, you are to ring the bell only when you feel the pains of childbirth." After saying this the king started on his journey. The six queens, who had overheard the king, went on the next day to the apartments of the seventh queen, and said, "What a nice bell of gold you have got, sister! Where did you get it, and why have you hung it up?" The seventh queen, in her simplicity, said, "The king has given it to me, and if I were to ring it, the king would immediately come to me wherever he might be at the time." "Impossible!" said the six queens, "you must have misunderstood the king. Who can believe that this bell can be heard at the distance of hundreds of miles? Besides, if it could be heard, how would the king be able to travel a great distance in the twinkling of an eye? This must be a hoax. If you ring the bell, you will find that what the king said was pure nonsense." The six queens then told her to make a trial. At first she was unwilling, remembering what the king had told her; but at last she was prevailed upon to ring the bell. The king was at the moment half-way to the capital of his other dominions, but at the ringing of the bell he stopped short in his journey, turned back, and in no time stood in the queen's apartments. Finding the queen going about in her rooms, he asked why she had rung the bell though her hour had not come. She, without informing the king of the entreaty of the six queens, replied that she rang the bell only to see whether what he had said was true. The king was somewhat indignant, told her distinctly not to ring the bell again till the moment of the coming upon her of the pains of childbirth, and then went away. After the lapse of some weeks the six queens again begged of the seventh queen to make a second trial of the bell. They said to her, "The first time when you rang the bell, the king was only at a short distance from you, it was therefore easy for him to hear the bell and to come to you; but now he has long ago settled in his other capital, let us see if he will now hear the bell and come to you." She resisted for a long time, but was at last prevailed upon by them to ring the bell. When the sound of the bell reached the king he was in court dispensing justice, but when he heard the sound of the bell (and no one else heard it) he closed the court and in no time stood in the queen's apartments. Finding that the queen was not about to be confined, he asked her why she had again rung the bell before her hour. She, without saying anything of the importunities of the six queens, replied that she merely made a second trial of the bell. The king became very angry, and said to her, "Now listen, since you have called me twice for nothing, let it be known to you that when the throes of childbirth do really come upon you, and you ring the bell ever so lustily, I will not come to you. You must be left to your fate." The king then went away.

At last the day of the seventh queen's deliverance arrived. On first feeling the pains she rang the golden bell. She waited, but the king did not make his appearance. She rang again with all her might, still the king did not make his appearance. The king certainly did hear the sound of the bell; but he did not come as he was displeased with the queen. When the six queens saw that the king did not come, they went to the seventh queen and told her that it was not customary with the ladies of the palace to be confined in the king's apartments; she must go to a hut near the stables. They then sent for the midwife of the palace, and heavily bribed her to make away with the infant the moment it should be born into the world. The seventh queen gave birth to a son who had the moon on his forehead and stars on the palms of his hands, and also to an uncommonly beautiful girl. The midwife had come provided with a couple of newly born pups. She put the pups before the mother, saying—"You have given birth to these," and took away the twin-children in an earthen vessel. The queen was quite insensible at the time, and did not notice the twins at the time they were carried away. The king, though he was angry with the seventh queen, yet remembering that she was destined to give birth to the heir of his throne, changed his mind, and came to see her the next morning. The pups were produced before the king as the offspring of the queen. The king's anger and vexation knew no bounds. He ordered that the seventh queen should be expelled from the palace, that she should be clothed in leather, and that she should be employed in the market-place to drive away crows and to keep off dogs. Though scarcely able to move she was driven away from the palace, stripped of her fine robes, clothed in leather, and set to drive away the crows of the market-place.

The midwife, when she put the twins in the earthen vessel, bethought herself of the best way to destroy them. She did not think it proper to throw them into a tank, lest they should be discovered the next day. Neither did she think of burying them in the ground, lest they should be dug up by a jackal and exposed to the gaze of people. The best way to make an end of them, she thought, would be to burn them, and reduce them to ashes, that no trace might be left of them. But how could she, at that dead hour of night, burn them without some other person helping her? A happy thought struck her. There was a potter on the outskirts of the city, who used during the day to mould vessels of clay on his wheel, and burn them during the latter part of the night. The midwife thought that the best plan would be to put the vessel with the twins along with the unburnt clay vessels which the potter had arranged in order and gone to sleep expecting to get up late at night and set them on fire; in this way, she thought, the twins would be reduced to ashes. She, accordingly, put the vessel with the twins along with the unburnt clay vessels of the potter, and went away.

Somehow or other, that night the potter and his wife overslept themselves. It was near the break of day when the potter's wife, awaking out of sleep, roused her husband, and said, "Oh, my good man, we have overslept ourselves; it is now near morning and I much fear it is now too late to set the pots on fire." Hastily unbolting the door of her cottage, she rushed out to the place where the pots were ranged in rows. She could scarcely believe her eyes when she saw that all the pots had been baked and were looking bright red, though neither she nor her husband had applied any fire to them. Wondering at her good luck, and not knowing what to make of it, she ran to her husband and said, "Just come and see!" The potter came, saw, and wondered. The pots had never before been so well baked. Who could have done this? This could have proceeded only from some god or goddess. Fumbling about the pots, he accidentally upturned one in which, lo and behold, were seen huddled up together two newly born infants of unearthly beauty. The potter said to his wife, "My dear, you must pretend to have given birth to these beautiful children." Accordingly all arrangements were made, and in due time it was given out that the twins had been born to her. And such lovely twins they were! On the same day many women of the neighbourhood came to see the potter's wife and the twins to which she had given birth, and to offer their congratulations on this unexpected good fortune. As for the potter's wife, she could not be too proud of her pretended children, and said to her admiring friends, "I had hardly hoped to have children at all. But now that the gods have given me these twins, may they receive the blessings of you all, and live for ever!"

The twins grew and were strengthened. The brother and sister, when they played about in the fields and lanes, were the admiration of every one who saw them; and all wondered at the uncommonly good luck of the potter in being blessed with such angelic children.

They were about twelve years old when the potter, their reputed father, became dangerously ill.

"A bright light, like that of the moon, was seen shining on his forehead"

It was evident to all that his sickness would end in death. The potter, perceiving his last end approaching, said to his wife, "My dear, I am going the way of all the earth; but I am leaving to you enough to live upon; live on and take care of these children." The woman said to her husband, "I am not going to survive you. Like all good and faithful wives, I am determined to die along with you. You and I will burn together on the same funeral pyre. As for the children, they are old enough to take care of themselves, and you are leaving them enough money." Her friends tried to dissuade her from her purpose, but in vain. The potter died; and as his remains were being burnt, his wife, now a widow, threw herself on the pyre, and burnt herself to death.

The boy with the moon on his forehead—by the way, he always kept his head covered with a turban lest the halo should attract notice—and his sister, now broke up the potter's establishment, sold the wheel and the pots and pans, and went to the bazaar in the king's city. The moment they entered, the bazaar was lit up on a sudden. The shopkeepers of the bazaar were greatly surprised. They thought some divine beings must have entered the place.

"The six queens tried to comfort him"

They looked upon the beautiful boy and his sister with wonder. They begged of them to stay in the bazaar. They built a house for them. When they used to ramble about, they were always followed at a distance by the woman clothed in leather, who was appointed by the king to drive away the crows of the bazaar.

By some unaccountable impulse she used also to hang about the house in which they lived. The boy in a short time bought a horse, and went a-hunting in the neighbouring forests. One day while he was hunting, the king was also hunting in the same forest, and seeing a brother huntsman the king drew near to him. The king was struck with the beauty of the lad and a yearning for him the moment he saw him. As a deer went past, the youth shot an arrow, and the reaction of the force necessary to shoot the arrow made the turban of his head fall off, on which a bright light, like that of the moon, was seen shining on his forehead. The king saw, and immediately thought of the son with the moon on his forehead and stars on the palms of his hands who was to have been born of his seventh queen. The youth on letting fly the arrow galloped off, in spite of the earnest entreaty of the king to wait and speak to him. The king went home a sadder man than he came out of it. He became very moody and melancholy. The six queens asked him why he was looking so sad. He told them that he had seen in the woods a lad with the moon on his forehead, which reminded him of the son who was to be born of the seventh queen. The six queens tried to comfort him in the best way they could; but they wondered who the youth could be. Was it possible that the twins were living? Did not the midwife say that she had burnt both the son and the daughter to ashes? Who, then, could this lad be? The midwife was sent for by the six queens and questioned. She swore that she had seen the twins burnt. As for the lad whom the king had met with, she would soon find out who he was. On making inquiries, the midwife soon found out that two strangers were living in the bazaar in a house which the shopkeepers had built for them. She entered the house and saw the girl only, as the lad had again gone out a-shooting. She pretended to be their aunt, who had gone away to another part of the country shortly after their birth; she had been searching after them for a long time, and was now glad to find them in the king's city near the palace. She greatly admired the beauty of the girl, and said to her, "My dear child, you are so beautiful, you require the kataki[1] flower properly to set off your beauty. You should tell your brother to plant a row of that flower in this courtyard." "What flower is that, auntie? I never saw it." "How could you have seen it, my child? It is not found here; it grows on the other side of the ocean, guarded by seven hundred Rakshasas." "How, then," said the girl, "will my brother get it?" "He may try to get it, if you speak to him," replied the woman. The woman made this proposal in the hope that the boy with the moon on his forehead would perish in the attempt to get the flower.

When the youth with the moon on his forehead returned from hunting, his sister told him of the visit paid to her by their aunt, and requested him, if possible, to get for her the kataki flower. He was sceptical about the existence of any aunt of theirs in the world, but he was resolved that, to please his beloved sister, he would get the flower on which she had set her heart. Next morning, accordingly, he started on his journey, after bidding his sister not to stir out of the house till his return. He rode on his fleet steed, which was of the pakshiraj[2] tribe, and soon reached the outskirts of what seemed to him dense forests of interminable length. He descried some Rakshasas prowling about. He went to some distance, shot with his arrows some deer and rhinoceroses in the neighbouring thickets, and, approaching the place where the Rakshasas were prowling about, called out, "O auntie dear, O auntie dear, your nephew is here." A huge Rakshasi came towards him and said, "O, you are the youth with the moon on your forehead and stars on the palms of your hands. We were all expecting you, but as you have called me aunt, I will not eat you up. What is it you want? Have you brought any eatables for me?" The youth gave her the deer and rhinoceroses which he had killed. Her mouth watered at the sight of the dead animals, and she began eating them. After swallowing down all the carcases, she said, "Well, what do you want?" The youth said, "I want some kataki flowers for my sister." She then told him that it would be difficult for him to get the flower, as it was guarded by seven hundred Rakshasas; however, he might make the attempt, but in the first instance he must go to his uncle on the north side of that forest. While the youth was going to his uncle of the north, on the way he killed some deer and rhinoceroses, and seeing a gigantic Rakshasa at some distance, cried out, "Uncle dear, uncle dear, your nephew is here. Auntie has sent me to you." The Rakshasa came near and said, "You are the youth with the moon on your forehead and stars on the palms of your hands; I would have swallowed you outright, had you not called me uncle, and had you not said that your aunt had sent you to me. Now, what is it you want?" The savoury deer and rhinoceroses were then presented to him; he ate them all, and then listened to the petition of the youth. The youth wanted the kataki flower. The Rakshasa said, "You want the kataki flower! Very well, try and get it if you can. After passing through this forest, you will come to an impenetrable forest of kachiri.[3] You will say to that forest, 'O mother kachiri! please make way for me, or else I die.' On that the forest will open up a passage for you. You will next come to the ocean. You will say to the ocean, 'O mother ocean! please make way for me, or else I die,' and the ocean will make way for you. After crossing the ocean, you enter the gardens where the kataki blooms. Good-bye; do as I have told you." The youth thanked his Rakshasa-uncle, and went on his way. After he had passed through the forest, he saw before him an impenetrable forest of kachiri. It was so close and thick, and withal so bristling with thorns, that not a mouse could go through it. Remembering the advice of his uncle, he stood before the forest with folded hands, and said, "O mother kachiri! please make way for me, or else I die." On a sudden a clean path was opened up in the forest, and the youth gladly passed through it. The ocean now lay before him. He said to the ocean, "O mother ocean! make way for me, or else I die." Forthwith the waters of the ocean stood up on two sides like two walls, leaving an open passage between them, and the youth passed through dryshod.

Now, right before him were the gardens of the kataki flower. He entered the inclosure, and found himself in a spacious palace which seemed to be unoccupied. On going from apartment to apartment he found a young lady of more than earthly beauty sleeping on a bedstead of gold. He went near, and noticed two little sticks, one of gold and the other of silver, lying in the bedstead. The silver stick lay near the feet of the sleeping beauty, and the golden one near the head. He took up the sticks in his hands, and as he was examining them, the golden stick accidentally fell upon the feet of the lady. In a moment the lady woke and sat up, and said to the youth, "Stranger, how have you come to this dismal place? I know who you are, and I know your history. You are the youth with the moon on your forehead and stars on the palms of your hands. Flee, flee from this place! This is the residence of seven hundred Rakshasas who guard the gardens of the kataki flower. They have all gone a-hunting; they will return by sundown; and if they find you here you will be eaten up. One Rakshasi brought me from the earth where my father is king. She loves me very dearly, and will not let me go away. By means of these gold and silver sticks she kills me when she goes away in the morning, and by means of those sticks she revives me when she returns in the evening. Flee, flee hence, or you die!" The youth told the young lady how his sister wished very much to have the kataki flower, how he passed through the forest of kachiri, and how he crossed the ocean. He said also that he was determined not to go alone, he must take the young lady along with him. The remaining part of the day they spent together in rambling about the gardens. As the time was drawing near when the Rakshasas should return, the youth buried himself amid an enormous heap of kataki flower which lay in an adjoining apartment, after killing the young lady by touching her head with the golden stick. Just after sunset the youth heard the sound as of a mighty tempest: it was the return of the seven hundred Rakshasas into the gardens. One of them entered the apartment of the young lady, revived her, and said, "I smell a human being, I smell a human being." The young lady replied, "How can a human being come to this place? I am the only human being here." The

Rakshasi then stretched herself on the floor, and told the young lady to shampoo her legs. As she was going on shampooing, she let fall a tear-drop on the Rakshasi's leg. "Why are you weeping, my dear child?" asked the raw-eater; "why are you weeping? Is anything troubling you?" "No, mamma," answered the young lady, "nothing is troubling me. What can trouble me, when you have made me so comfortable? I was only thinking what will become of me when you die." "When I die, child?" said the Rakshasi; "shall I die? Yes, of course all creatures die; but the death of a Rakshasa or Rakshasi will never happen. You know, child, that deep tank in the middle part of these gardens. Well, at the bottom of that tank there is a wooden box, in which there are a male and a female bee. It is ordained by fate that if a human being who has the moon on his forehead and stars on the palms of his hands were to come here and dive into that tank, and get hold of the same wooden box, and crush to death the male and female bees without letting a drop of their blood fall to the ground, then we should die. But the accomplishment of this decree of fate is, I think, impossible. For, in the first place, there can be no such human being who will have the moon on his forehead and stars on the palms of his hands; and, in the second place, if there be such a man, he will find it impossible to come to this place, guarded as it is by seven hundred of us, encompassed by a deep ocean, and barricaded by an impervious forest of kachiri—not to speak of the outposts and sentinels that are stationed on the other side of the forest. And then, even if he succeeds in coming here, he will perhaps not know the secret of the wooden box; and even if he knows of the secret of the wooden box, he may not succeed in killing the bees without letting a drop of their blood fall on the ground. And woe be to him if a drop does fall on the ground, for in that case he will be torn up into seven hundred pieces by us. You see then, child, that we are almost immortal—not actually, but virtually so. You may, therefore, dismiss your fears."

On the next morning the Rakshasi got up, killed the young lady by means of the sticks, and went away in search of food along with other Rakshasas and Rakshasis. The lad, who had the moon on his forehead and stars on the palms of his hands, came out of the heap of flowers and revived the young lady. The young lady recited to the young man the whole of the conversation she had had with the Rakshasi. It was a perfect revelation to him. He, however, lost no time in beginning to act. He shut the heavy gates of the gardens. He dived into the tank and brought up the wooden box. He opened the wooden box, and caught hold of the male and female bees as they were about to escape. He crushed them on the palms of his hands, besmearing his body with every drop of their blood. The moment this was done, loud cries and groans were heard around about the inclosure of the gardens. Agreeably to the decree of fate all the Rakshasas approached the gardens and fell down dead. The youth with the moon on his forehead took as many kataki flowers as he could, together with their seeds, and left the palace, around which were lying in mountain heaps the carcases of the mighty dead, in company with the young and beautiful lady. The waters of the ocean retreated before the youth as before, and the forest of kachiri also opened up a passage through it; and the happy couple reached the house in the bazaar, where they were welcomed by the sister of the youth who had the moon on his forehead.

On the following morning the youth, as usual, went to hunt. The king was also there. A deer passed by, and the youth shot an arrow. As he shot, the turban as usual fell off his head, and a bright light issued from it. The king saw and wondered. He told the youth to stop, as he wished to contract friendship with him. The youth told him to come to his house, and gave him his address. The king went to the house of the youth in the middle of the day. Pushpavati—for that was the name of the young lady that had been brought from beyond the ocean—told the king—for she knew the whole history—how his seventh queen had been persuaded by the other six queens to ring the bell twice before her time, how she was delivered of a beautiful boy and girl, how pups were substituted in their room, how the twins were saved in a miraculous manner in the house of the potter, how they were well treated in the bazaar, and how the youth with the moon on his forehead rescued her from the clutches of the Rakshasas. The king, mightily incensed with the six queens, had them, on the following day, buried alive in the ground. The seventh queen was then brought from the market-place and reinstated in her position; and the youth with the moon on his forehead, and the lovely Pushpavati and their sister, lived happily together.

1. Calotropis gigantea.
2. Literally the king of birds, a fabulous species of horse remarkable for their swiftness.
3. Arum fornicatum.

5

The Ghost who was Afraid of being Bagged

Once on a time there lived a barber who had a wife. They did not live happily together, as the wife always complained that she had not enough to eat. Many were the curtain lectures which were inflicted upon the poor barber. The wife used often to say to her mate, "If you had not the means to support a wife, why did you marry me? People who have not means ought not to indulge in the luxury of a wife. When I was in my father's house I had plenty to eat, but it seems that I have come to your house to fast. Widows only fast; I have become a widow in your life-time." She was not content with mere words; she got very angry one day and struck her husband with the broomstick of the house. Stung with shame, and abhorring himself on account of his wife's reproach and beating, he left his house, with the implements of his craft, and vowed never to return and see his wife's face again till he had become rich. He went from village to village, and towards nightfall came to the outskirts of a forest. He laid himself down at the foot of a tree, and spent many a sad hour in bemoaning his hard lot.

"Now, barber, I am going to destroy you. Who will protect you?"

It so chanced that the tree, at the foot of which the barber was lying down, was dwelt in by a ghost. The ghost seeing a human being at the foot of the tree naturally thought of destroying him. With this intention the ghost alighted from the tree, and, with outspread arms and a gaping mouth, stood like a tall palmyra tree before the barber, and said, "Now, barber, I am going to destroy you. Who will protect you?" The barber, though quaking in every limb through fear, and his hair standing erect, did not lose his presence of mind, but, with that promptitude and shrewdness which are characteristic of his fraternity, replied, "O spirit, you will destroy me! wait a bit and I'll show you how many ghosts I have captured this very night and put into my bag; and right glad am I to find you here, as I shall have one more ghost in my bag." So saying the barber produced from his bag a small looking-glass, which he always carried about with him along with his razors, his whetstone, his strop and other utensils, to enable his customers to see whether their beards had been well shaved or not. He stood up, placed the looking-glass right against the face of the ghost, and said, "Here you see one ghost which I have seized and bagged; I am going to put you also in the bag to keep this ghost company." The ghost, seeing his own face in the looking-glass, was convinced of the truth of what the barber had said, and was filled with fear. He said to the barber, "O, sir barber, I'll do whatever you bid me, only do not put me into your bag. I'll give you whatever you want." The barber said, "You ghosts are a faithless set, there is no trusting you. You will promise, and not give what you promise." "O, sir," replied the ghost, "be merciful to me; I'll bring to you whatever you order; and if I do not bring it, then put me into your bag." "Very well," said the barber, "bring me just now one thousand gold mohurs; and by to-morrow night you must raise a granary in my house, and fill it with paddy. Go and get the gold mohurs immediately: and if you fail to do my bidding you will certainly be put into my bag." The ghost gladly consented to the conditions. He went away, and in the course of a short time returned with a bag containing a thousand gold mohurs. The barber was delighted beyond measure at the sight of the gold mohurs. He then told the ghost to see to it that by the following night a granary was erected in his house and filled with paddy.

It was during the small hours of the morning that the barber, loaded with the heavy treasure, knocked at the door of his house. His wife, who reproached herself for having in a fit of rage struck her husband with a broomstick, got out of bed and unbolted the door. Her surprise was great when she saw her husband pour out of the bag a glittering heap of gold mohurs.

The next night the poor devil, through fear of being bagged, raised a large granary in the barber's house, and spent the live-long night in carrying on his back large packages of paddy till the granary was filled up to the brim. The uncle of this terrified ghost, seeing his worthy nephew carrying on his back loads of paddy, asked what the matter was. The ghost related what had happened. The uncle-ghost then said, "You fool, you think the barber can bag you! The barber is a cunning fellow; he has cheated you, like a simpleton as you are." "You doubt," said the nephew-ghost, "the power of the barber! come and see." The uncle-ghost then went to the barber's house, and peeped into it through a window. The barber, perceiving from the blast of wind which the arrival of the ghost had produced that a ghost was at the window, placed full before it the self-same looking-glass, saying, "Come now, I'll put you also into the bag." The uncle-ghost, seeing his own face in the looking-glass, got quite frightened, and promised that very night to raise another granary and to fill it, not this time with paddy, but with rice. So in two nights the barber became a rich man, and lived happily with his wife begetting sons and daughters.

6

The Field of Bones

nce on a time there lived a king who had a son. The young prince had three friends, the son of the prime minister, the son of the prefect of the police, and the son of the richest merchant of the city. These four friends had great love for one another. Once on a time they bethought themselves of seeing distant lands. They accordingly set out one day, each one riding on a horse. They rode on and on, till about noon they came to the outskirts of what seemed to be a dense forest. There they rested a while, tying to the trees their horses, which began to browse. When they had refreshed themselves, they again mounted their horses and resumed their journey. At sunset they saw in the depths of the forest a temple, near which they dismounted, wishing to lodge there that night. Inside the temple there was a sannyasi,[1] apparently absorbed in meditation, as he did not notice the four friends. When darkness covered the forest, a light was seen inside the temple. The four friends resolved to pass the night on the balcony of the temple; and as the forest was infested with many wild beasts, they deemed it safe that each of them should watch one prahara[2] of the night, while the rest should sleep. It fell to the lot of the merchant's son to watch during the first prahara, that is to say, from six in the evening to nine o'clock at night. Towards the end of his watch the merchant's son saw a wonderful sight. The hermit took up a bone with his hand, and repeated over it some words which the merchant's son distinctly heard. The moment the words were uttered, a clattering sound was heard in the precincts of the temple, and the merchant's son saw many bones moving from different parts of the forest. The bones collected themselves inside the temple, at the foot of the hermit, and lay there in a heap. As soon as this took place, the watch of the merchant's son came to an end; and, rousing the son of the prefect of the police, he laid himself down to sleep.

The prefect's son, when he began his watch, saw the hermit sitting cross-legged, wrapped in meditation, near a heap of bones, the history of which he, of course, did not know. For a long time nothing happened. The dead stillness of the night was broken only by the howl of the hyæna and the wolf, and the growl of the tiger. When his time was nearly up he saw a wonderful sight. The hermit looked at the heap of bones lying before him, and uttered some words which the prefect's son distinctly heard. No sooner had the words been uttered than a noise was heard among the bones, "and behold a shaking, and the bones came together, bone to its bone"; and the bones which were erewhile lying together in a heap now took the form of a skeleton. Struck with wonder, the prefect's son would have watched longer, but his time was over. He therefore laid himself down to sleep, after rousing the minister's son, to whom, however, he told nothing of what he had seen, as the merchant's son had not told him anything of what he had seen.

The minister's son got up, rubbed his eyes, and began watching. It was the dead hour of midnight, when ghosts, hobgoblins, and spirits of every name and description, go roaming over the wide world, and when all creation, both animate and inanimate, is in deep repose. Even the howl of the wolf and the hyæna and the growl of the tiger had ceased. The minister's son looked towards the temple, and saw the hermit sitting wrapt up in meditation; and near him lying something which seemed to be the skeleton of some animal. He looked towards the dense forest and the darkness all around, and his hair stood on end through terror. In this state of fear and trembling he spent nearly three hours, when an uncommon sight in the temple attracted his notice. The hermit, looking at the skeleton before him, uttered some words which the minister's son distinctly heard. As soon as the words were uttered, "lo, the sinews and the flesh came up upon the bones, and the skin covered them above"; but there was no breath in the skeleton. Astonished at the sight, the minister's son would have sat up longer, but his time was up. He therefore laid himself down to sleep, after having roused the king's son, to whom, however, he said nothing of what he had seen and heard.

The king's son, when he began his watch, saw the hermit sitting, completely absorbed in devotion, near a figure which looked like some animal, but he was not a little surprised to see the animal lying apparently lifeless, without showing any of the symptoms of life. The prince spent his hours agreeably enough, especially as he had had a long sleep, and as he felt none of that depression which the dead hour of midnight sheds on the spirits; and he amused himself with marking how the shades of darkness were becoming thinner and paler every moment. But just as he noticed a red streak in the east, he heard a sound from inside the temple. He turned his eyes towards the hermit. The hermit, looking towards the inanimate figure of the animal lying before him, uttered some words which the prince distinctly heard. The moment the words were spoken, "breath came into the animal; it lived, it stood up upon its feet"; and quickly rushed out of the temple into the forest. That moment the crows cawed; the watch of the prince came to an end; his three companions were roused; and after a short time they mounted their horses, and resumed their journey, each one thinking of the strange sight seen in the temple.

They rode on and on through the dense and interminable forest, and hardly spoke to one another, till about mid-day they halted under a tree near a pool for refreshment. After they had refreshed themselves with eating some fruits of the forest and drinking water from the pool, the prince said to his three companions, "Friends, did you not see something in the temple of the devotee? I'll tell you what I saw, but first let me hear what you all saw. Let the merchant's son first tell us what he saw as he had the first watch; and the others will follow in order."

Merchant's son. I'll tell you what I saw. I saw the hermit take up a bone in his hand, and repeat some words which I well remember. The moment those words were uttered, a clattering sound was heard in the precincts of the temple, and I saw many bones running into the temple from different directions. The bones collected themselves together inside the temple at the feet of the hermit, and lay there in a heap. I would have gladly remained longer to see the end, but my time was up, and I had to rouse my friend, the son of the prefect of the police.

Prefect's son. Friends, this is what I saw. The hermit looked at the heap of bones lying before him, and uttered some words which I well remember. No sooner had the words been uttered than I heard a noise among the bones, and, strange to say, the bones jumped up, each bone joined itself to its fellow, and the heap became a perfect skeleton. At that moment my watch came to an end, and I had to rouse my respected friend the minister's son.

Minister's son. Well, when I began my watch I saw the said skeleton lying near the hermit. After three mortal hours, during which I was in great fear, I saw the hermit lift his eyes towards the skeleton and utter some words which I well remember. As soon as the words were uttered the skeleton was covered with flesh and hair, but it did not show any symptom of life, as it lay motionless. Just then my watch ended, and I had to rouse my royal friend the prince.

King's son. Friends, from what you yourselves saw, you can guess what I saw. I saw the hermit turn towards the skeleton covered with skin and hair, and repeat some words which I well remember. The moment the words were uttered, the skeleton stood up on its feet, and it looked a fine and lusty deer, and while I was admiring its beauty, it skipped out of the temple, and ran into the forest. That moment the crows cawed.

The four friends, after hearing one another's story, congratulated themselves on the possession of supernatural power, and they did not doubt but that if they pronounced the words which they had heard the hermit utter, the utterance would be followed by the same results. But they resolved to verify their power by an actual experiment. Near the foot of the tree they found a bone lying on the ground, and they accordingly resolved to experiment upon it. The merchant's son took up the bone, and repeated over it the formula he had heard from the hermit. Wonderful to relate, a hundred bones immediately came rushing from different directions, and lay in a heap at the foot of the tree. The son of the prefect of the police then looking upon the heap of bones, repeated the formula which he had heard from the hermit, and forthwith there was a shaking among the bones; the several bones joined themselves together, and formed themselves into a skeleton, and it was the skeleton of a quadruped. The minister's son then drew near the skeleton, and, looking intently upon it, pronounced over it the formula which he had heard from the hermit. The skeleton immediately was covered with flesh, skin, and hair, and, horrible to relate, the animal proved itself to be a royal tiger of the largest size. The four friends were filled with consternation. If the king's son were, by the repetition of the formula he had heard from the hermit, to make the beast alive, it might prove fatal to them all. The three friends, therefore, tried to dissuade the prince from giving life to the tiger. But the prince would not comply with the request. He naturally said, "The mantras[3] which you have learned have been proved true and efficacious. But how shall I know that the mantra which I have learned is equally efficacious? I must have my mantra verified. Nor is it certain that we shall lose our lives by the experiment. Here is this high tree. You can climb into its topmost branches, and I shall also follow you thither after pronouncing the mantra."

In vain did the three friends dwell upon the extreme danger attending the experiment: the prince remained inexorable. The minister's son, the prefect's son, and the merchant's son climbed up into the topmost branches of the tree, while the king's son went up to the middle of the tree. From there, looking intently upon the lifeless tiger, he pronounced the words which he had learned from the hermit, and quickly ran up the tree. In the twinkling of an eye the tiger stood upright, gave out a terrible growl, with a tremendous spring killed all the four horses which were browsing at a little distance, and, dragging one of them, rushed towards the densest part of the forest. The four friends ensconced on the branches of the tree were almost petrified with fear at the sight of the terrible tiger; but the danger was now over. The tiger went off at a great distance from them, and from its growl they judged that it must be at least two miles distance from them. After a little they came down from the tree; and as they now had no horses on which to ride, they walked on foot through the forest, till, coming to its end, they reached the shore of the sea. They sat on the sea-shore hoping to see some ship sailing by. They had not sat long, when fortunately they descried a vessel in the offing. They waved their handkerchiefs, and made all sorts of signs to attract the notice of the people on board the ship. The captain and the crew noticed the men on the shore. They came towards the shore, took the men upon board, but added that as they were short of provisions they could not have them a long time on board, but would put them ashore at the first port they came to. After four or five days' voyage, they saw not far from the shore high buildings and turrets, and supposing the place to be a large city, the four friends landed there.

"They approached a magnificent pile of buildings"

The four friends, immediately after landing, walked along a long avenue of stately trees, at the end of which was a bazaar. There were hundreds of shops in the bazaar, but not a single human being in them. There were sweetmeat shops in which there were heaps of confectioneries ranged in regular rows, but no human beings to sell them. There was the blacksmith's shop, there was the anvil, there were the bellows and the other tools of the smithy, but there was no smith there. There were stalls in which there were heaps of faded and dried vegetables, but no men or women to sell them. The streets were all deserted, no human beings, no cattle were to be seen there. There were carts, but no bullocks; there were carriages, but no horses. The doors and windows of the houses of the city on both sides of the streets were all open, but no human being was visible in them. It seemed to be a deserted city. It seemed to be a city of the dead—and all the dead taken out and buried. The four friends were astonished—they were frightened at the sight. As they went on, they approached a magnificent pile of buildings, which seemed to be the palace of a king. They went to the gate and to the porter's lodge. They saw shields, swords, spears, and other weapons suspended in the lodge, but no porters. They entered the premises, but saw no guards, no human beings. They went to the stables, saw the troughs, grain, and grass lying about in profusion, but no horses. They went inside the palace, passed the long corridors—still no human being was visible. They went through six long courts—still no human being. They entered the seventh court, and there and then, for the first time, did they see living human beings. They saw coming towards them four princesses of matchless beauty. Each of these four princesses caught hold of the arm of each of the four friends; and each princess called each man whom she had caught hold of her husband. The princesses said that they had been long waiting for the four friends, and expressed great joy at their arrival. The princesses took the four friends into the innermost apartments, and gave them a sumptuous feast. There were no servants attending them, the princesses themselves bringing in the provisions and setting them before the four friends. At the outset the four princesses told the four friends that no questions were to be asked about the depopulation of the city. After this, each princess went into her private apartment along with her newly-found husband. Shortly after the prince and princess had retired into their private apartment, the princess began to shed tears. On the prince inquiring into the cause, the princess said, "O prince! I pity you very much. You seem, by your bearing, to be the son of a king, and you have, no doubt, the heart of a king's son; I will therefore tell you my whole story, and the story of my three companions who look like princesses. I am the daughter of a king, whose palace this is, and those three creatures, who are dressed like princesses, and who have called your three friends their husbands, are Rakshasis. They came to this city some time ago; they ate up my father, the king, my mother, the queen, my brothers, my sisters, of whom I had a large number. They ate up the king's ministers and servants. They ate up gradually all the people of the city, all my father's horses and elephants, and all the cattle of the city. You must have noticed, as you came to the palace, that there are no human beings, no cattle, no living thing in this city. They have all been eaten up by those three Rakshasis. They have spared me alone—and that, I suppose, only for a time. When the Rakshasis saw you and your friends from a distance, they were very glad, as they mean to eat you all up after a short time."

King's son. But if this is the case, how do I know that you are not a Rakshasi yourself? Perhaps you mean to swallow me up by throwing me off my guard.

Princess. I'll mention one fact which proves that those three creatures are Rakshasis, while I am not. Rakshasis, you know, eat food a hundred times larger in quantity than men or women. What the Rakshasis eat at table along with us is not sufficient to appease their hunger. They therefore go out at night to distant lands in search of men or cattle, as there are none in this city.

If you ask your friends to watch and see whether their wives remain all night in their beds, they will find they go out and stay away a good part of the night, whereas you will find me the whole night with you. But please see that the Rakshasis do not get the slightest inkling of all this; for if they hear of it, they will kill me in the first instance, and afterwards swallow you all up.

The next day the king's son called together the minister's son, the prefect's son, and the merchant's son, and held a consultation, enjoining the strictest secrecy on all. He told them what he had heard from the princess, and requested them to lie awake in their beds to watch whether their pretended princesses went out at night or not. One presumptive argument in favour of the assertion of the princess was that all the pretended princesses were fast asleep during the whole of the day in consequence of their nightly wanderings, whereas the female friend of the king's son did not sleep at all during the day. The three friends accordingly lay in their beds at night pretending to be asleep and manifesting all the symptoms of deep sleep. Each one observed that his female friend at a certain hour, thinking her mate to be in deep sleep, left the room, stayed away the whole night, and returned to her bed only at dawn. During the following day each female friend slept out nearly the whole day, and woke up only in the afternoon. For two nights and days the three friends observed this. The king's son also remained awake at night pretending to be asleep, but the princess was not observed for a single moment to leave the room, nor was she observed to sleep in the day. From these circumstances the friends of the king's son began to suspect that their partners were really Rakshasis as the princess said they were.

By way of confirmation the princess also told the king's son, that the Rakshasis, after eating the flesh of men and animals, threw the bones towards the north of the city, where there was an immense collection of them. The king's son and his three friends went one day towards that part of the city, and sure enough they saw there immense heaps of the bones of men and animals piled up into hills. From this they became more and more convinced that the three women were Rakshasis in deed and truth.

The question now was how to run away from these devourers of men and animals? There was one circumstance greatly in favour of the four friends, and that was, that the three Rakshasis slept during nearly the whole day; they had therefore the greater part of the day for the maturing of their plans. The princess advised them to go towards the sea-shore, and watch if any ships sailed that way. The four friends accordingly used to go to the sea-shore looking for ships. They were always accompanied by the princess, who took the precaution of carrying with her in a bundle her most valuable jewels, pearls and precious stones. It happened one day that they saw a ship passing at a great distance from the shore. They made signs which attracted the notice of the captain and crew. The ship came towards the land, and the four friends and princess were, after much entreaty, taken up. The princess exhorted the crew to row with all their might, for which she promised them a handsome reward; for she knew that the Rakshasis would awake in the afternoon, and immediately come after the ship; and they would assuredly catch hold of the vessel and destroy all the crew and passengers if it stood short of eighty miles from land, for the Rakshasis had the power of distending their bodies to the length of ten

Yojanas.[4] The four friends and the princess cheered on the crew, and the oarsmen rowed with all their might; and the ship, favoured by the wind, shot over the deep like lightning. It was near sun-down when a terrible yell was heard on the shore. The Rakshasis had wakened from their sleep, and not finding either the four friends or the princess, naturally thought they had got hold of a ship and were escaping. They therefore ran along the shore with lightning rapidity, and seeing the ship afar off they distended their bodies. But fortunately the vessel was more than eighty miles off land, though only a trifle more: indeed, the ship was so dangerously near that the heads of the Rakshasis with their widely-distended jaws almost touched its stern. The words which the Rakshasis uttered in the hearing of the crew and passengers were—"O sister, so you are going to eat them all yourself alone." The minister's son, the prefect's son, and the merchant's son had all along a suspicion that the pretended princess, the prince's partner, might after all also be a Rakshasi; that suspicion was now confirmed by what they heard the three Rakshasis say. Those words, however, produced no effect in the mind of the king's son, as from his intimate acquaintance with the princess he could not possibly take her to be a Rakshasi.

The captain told the four friends and princess that as he was bound for distant regions in search of gold mines, he could not take them along with him; he, therefore, proposed that on the next day he should put them ashore near some port, especially as they were now safe from the clutches of the Rakshasis. On the following day no port was visible for a long time; towards the evening, however, they came near a port where the four friends and the princess were landed. After walking some distance, the princess, who had never been accustomed to take long walks, complained of fatigue and hunger; they all therefore sat under a tree, and the king's son sent the merchant's son to buy some sweetmeats in the bazaar which they heard was not far off. The merchant's son did not return, as he was fully persuaded in his mind that the king's son's partner was as real a Rakshasi as the three others from whose clutches he had escaped. Seeing the delay of the merchant's son, the king's son sent the prefect's son after him; but neither did he return, he being also convinced that the pretended princess was a Rakshasi. The minister's son was next sent; but he also joined the other two. The king's son then himself went to the shop of the sweetmeat seller where he met his three friends, who made him remain with them by main force, earnestly declaring that the woman was no princess, but a real Rakshasi like the other three. Thus the princess was deserted by the four friends who returned to their own country, full of the adventures they had met with.

In the meantime the princess walked to the bazaar and found shelter for a few days in the house of a poor woman, after which she set out for the city of the four friends, the name and whereabouts of which city she had learnt from the king's son. On arriving at the city, she sold some of her costly ornaments, pearls and precious stones, and hired a stately house for her residence with a suitable establishment.

"Thus the princess was deserted"

She caused herself to be proclaimed as a heaven-born dice-player, and challenged all the players in the city to play, the conditions of the game being that if she lost it she would give the winner a lakh[5] of rupees, and if she won it she should get a lakh from him who lost the game. She also got authority from the king of the country to imprison in her own house any one who could not pay her the stipulated sum of money.

The merchant's son, the prefect's son, and the minister's son, who all looked upon themselves as miraculous players, played with the princess, paid her many lakhs, but being unable to pay her all the sums they owed her, were imprisoned in her house. At last the king's son offered to play with her. The princess purposely allowed him to win the first game, which emboldened him to play many times, in all of which he was the loser; and being unable to pay the many lakhs owing her, the prince was about to be dragged into the dungeon, when the princess told him who she was. The merchant's son, the prefect's son, and the minister's son were brought out of their cells; and the joy of the four friends knew no bounds. The king and the queen received their daughter-in-law with open arms, and with demonstrations of great festivity.

Every one in the palace was glad except the princess. She could not forget that her parents, her brothers and sisters had been devoured by the Rakshasis, and that their bones, along with the bones of her father's subjects, stood in mountain heaps on the north side of the capital. The prince had told her that he and his three friends had the power of giving life to bones. They could then reconstruct the frames of her parents and other relatives; but the difficulty lay in this—how to kill the three Rakshasis. Could not the hermit, who taught them to give life, not teach also how to take away life? In all likelihood he could. Reasoning in this manner, the four friends and the princess went to the temple of the hermit in the forest, prayed to him to give them the secret of destroying life from a distance by a charm. The hermit became propitious, and granted the boon. A deer was passing by at the moment. The hermit took a handful of water, repeated over it some words which the king's son distinctly heard, and threw it upon the deer. The deer died in a moment. He repeated other words over the dead animal, the deer jumped up and ran away into the forest.

Armed with this killing charm, the king's son, together with the princess and the three friends, went to his father-in-law's capital. As they approached the city of death, the three Rakshasis ran furiously towards them with open jaws. The king's son spilled charmed water upon them, and they died in an instant. They all then went to the heaps of bones. The merchant's son brought together the proper bones of the bodies, the prefect's son constructed them into skeletons, the minister's son clothed them with sinews, flesh, and skin, and the king's son gave them life. The princess was entranced at the sight of the re-animation of her parents and other relatives, and her eyes were filled with tears of joy. After a few days which they spent in great festivity, they left the revivified city, went to their own country, and lived many years in great happiness.

1. Religious devotee.
2. Eighth part of twenty-four hours, that is, three hours.
3. Charm or incantation.
4. A yojana is nearly eight miles.
5. Ten thousand pounds sterling.

7

The Bald Wife

A certain man had two wives, the younger of whom he loved more than the elder. The younger wife had two tufts of hair on her head, and the elder only one. The man went to a distant town for merchandise; so the two wives lived together in the house. But they hated each other: the younger one, who was her husband's favourite, ill-treated the other. She made her do all the menial work in the house; rebuked her all day and night; and did not give her enough to eat. One day the younger wife said to the elder, "Come and take away all the lice from the hair of my head." While the elder wife was searching among the younger one's hair for the vermin, one lock of hair by chance gave way; on which the younger one, mightily incensed, tore off the single tuft that was on the head of the elder wife, and drove her away from the house. The elder wife, now become completely bald, determined to go into the forest, and there either die of starvation or be devoured by some wild beast. On her way she passed by a cotton plant. She stopped near it, made for herself a broom with some sticks which lay about, and swept clean the ground round about the plant. The plant was much pleased, and gave her a blessing. She wended on her way, and now saw a plantain tree. She swept the ground round about the plantain tree which, being pleased with her, gave her a blessing. As she went on she saw the shed of a Brahmani bull. As the shed was very dirty, she swept the place clean, on which the bull, being much pleased, blessed her. She next saw a tulasi plant, bowed herself down before it, and cleaned the place round about, on which the plant gave her a blessing. As she was going on in her journey she saw a hut made of branches of trees and leaves, and near it a man sitting cross-legged, apparently absorbed in meditation. She stood for a moment behind the venerable muni. "Whoever you may be," he said, "come before me; do not stand behind me; if you do, I will reduce you to ashes." The woman, trembling with fear, stood before the muni. "What is your petition?" asked the muni. "Father Muni," answered the woman, "thou knowest how miserable I am, since thou art all-knowing. My husband does not love me, and his other wife, having torn off the only tuft of hair on my head, has driven me away from the house. Have pity upon me, Father Muni!" The muni, continuing sitting, said, "Go into the tank which you see yonder. Plunge into the water only once, and then come to me again." The woman went to the tank, washed in it, and plunged into the water only once, according to the bidding of the muni. When she got out of the water, what a change was seen in her! Her head was full of jet black hair, which was so long that it touched her heels; her complexion had become perfectly fair; and she looked young and beautiful.

*"When she got out of the water, what a change was
seen in her!"*

Filled with joy and gratitude, she went to the muni, and bowed
herself to the ground. The muni said to her, "Rise, woman. Go
inside the hut, and you will find a number of wicker baskets,
and bring out any you like." The woman went into the hut, and
selected a modest-looking basket. The muni said, "Open the

basket." She opened it, and found it filled with ingots of gold, pearls and all sorts of precious stones. The muni said, "Woman, take that basket with you. It will never get empty. When you take away the present contents their room will be supplied by another set, and that by another, and that by another, and the basket will never become empty. Daughter, go in peace." The woman bowed herself down to the ground in profound but silent gratitude, and went away.

As she was returning homewards with the basket in her hand, she passed by the tulasi plant whose bottom she had swept. The tulasi plant said to her, "Go in peace, child! thy husband will love thee warmly." She next came to the shed of the Brahmani bull, who gave her two shell ornaments which were twined round its horns, saying, "Daughter, take these shells, put them on your wrists, and whenever you shake either of them you will get whatever ornaments you wish to obtain." She then came to the plantain tree, which gave her one of its broad leaves, saying, "Take, child, this leaf; and when you move it you will get not only all sorts of delicious plantains, but all kinds of agreeable food." She came last of all to the cotton plant, which gave her one of its own branches, saying, "Daughter, take this branch; and when you shake it you will get not only all sorts of cotton clothes, but also of silk and purple. Shake it now in my presence." She shook the branch, and a fabric of the finest glossy silk fell on her lap. She put on that silk cloth, and wended on her way with the shells on her wrists, and the basket and the branch and the leaf in her hands.

The younger wife was standing at the door of her house, when she saw a beautiful woman approach her. She could scarcely believe her eyes. What a change! The old, bald hag turned into the very Queen of Beauty herself! The elder wife, now grown rich and beautiful, treated the younger wife with kindness. She gave her fine clothes, costly ornaments, and the richest viands. But all to no purpose. The younger wife envied the beauty and hair of her associate. Having heard that she got it all from Father Muni in the forest, she determined to go there. Accordingly she started on her journey. She saw the cotton plant, but did nothing to it; she passed by the plantain tree, the shed of the Brahmani bull, and the tulasi plant, without taking any notice of them. She approached the muni. The muni told her to bathe in the tank, and plunge only once into the water. She gave one plunge, at which she got a glorious head of hair and a beautifully fair complexion. She thought a second plunge would make her still more beautiful. Accordingly she plunged into the water again, and came out as bald and ugly as before. She came to the muni, and wept. The sage drove her away, saying, "Be off, you disobedient woman. You will get no boon from me." She went back to her house mad with grief. The lord of the two women returned from his travels and was struck with the long locks and beauty of his first wife. He loved her dearly; and when he saw her secret and untold resources and her incredible wealth, he almost adored her. They lived together happily for many years, and had for their maid-servant the younger woman, who had been formerly his best beloved.

"Why, O Natiya-thorn, dost wither?"
"Why does thy cow on me browse?"
"Why, O cow, dost thou browse?"

"Why does thy neat-herd not tend me?"
"Why, O neat-herd, dost not tend the cow?"
"Why does thy daughter-in-law not give me rice?"
"Why, O daughter-in-law, dost not give rice?"
"Why does my child cry?"
"Why, O child, dost thou cry?"
"Why does the ant bite me?"
"Why, O ant, dost thou bite?"
Koot! koot! koot!

❏❏❏

www.ingramcontent.com/pod-product-compliance
Lightning Source LLC
Chambersburg PA
CBHW060448160726
47992CB00003B/1127